JOSEPH'S GRACE

ALSO BY SHELIA P. MOSES

JOSEPH'S GRACE

SHELIA P. MOSES

Margaret K. McElderry Books

New York London Toronto Sydney

MARGARET K. McELDERRY BOOKS
An imprint of Simon & Schuster Children's Publishing Division
1230 Avenue of the Americas, New York, New York 10020
MARGARET K. McELDERRY BOOKS is a trademark of Simon & Schuster, Inc.
For information about special discounts for bulk purchases, please contact Simon & Schuster
Special Sales at 1-866-506-1949 or business@simonandschuster.com.
The Simon & Schuster Speakers Bureau can bring authors to your live event. For more
information or to book an event, contact the Simon & Schuster Speakers Bureau at
1-866-248-3049 or visit our website at www.simonspeakers.com.
Book edited by Emma D. Dryden
The text for this book is set in Adobe Garamond.
Manufactured in the United States of America
10 9 8 7 6 5 4 3 2 1
Library of Congress Cataloging-in-Publication Data
Moses, Shelia P.
Joseph's grace / Shelia P. Moses.—1st ed.
p.   cm.
Sequel to: Joseph.
Summary: Now a high school junior, Joseph Flood contends with grief over his late cousin
Jasmine, his mother's addictions and pleas for money, the distance between himself and his
father in Iraq, making the tennis team, and a new relationship.
ISBN 978-1-4169-3942-9 (hardcover)
ISBN 978-1-4424-0618-6 (eBook)
[1. Family problems—Fiction. 2. Mothers—Fiction. 3. Alcoholism—Fiction.
4. Drug abuse—Fiction. 5. Grief—Fiction. 6. African Americans—Fiction.] I. Title.
PZ7.M8475Jq 2011
[Fic]—dc22
2009048965

For Emma Dryden—
You are a wonderful editor
and a great friend.
Let it rain!

CHAPTER ONE

"Amaaaaaazing grace! How sweet the sound

That saved a wretch like me!

I once was lost,

But now am found,

Was blind, but now I seeeee."

Miss Novella Edmonds sings as everyone screams and cries at my cousin Jasmine's funeral.

"Help me, Jesus," she says, and makes her way back to her seat in the choir stand after singing and shouting all over the place.

"Help me, Lord. Help me," she says between verses as Miss Fitten fans her with the paper fan that has a picture of Martin Luther King Jr. and his family on it. Miss Fitten is crying and shouting too.

I have never seen a dead person look so pretty. My cousin Jasmine looks like an angel lying in her white casket. The pink lace lining matches her pink, green, and white dress. She called that dress her AKA sorority outfit. Jasmine bought the dress on sale at Macy's in Crabtree Valley Mall over in Raleigh, and she was saving it to wear to the end-of-the-summer dance on North Carolina Central University's campus, two weeks from now. My cousin was treating herself after making all A's her senior year in college. She was so excited about starting graduate school at NCCU in the fall. I was excited for her. We all were.

Poor Jasmine had no idea she was buying a dress for her own funeral. She had no idea she wouldn't live long enough to go to the dance or attend graduate school in the fall. I had no idea my cousin would die so young.

Jasmine was just doing what she did best. She was planning ahead. Jasmine always wanted to be ready for the next exciting thing that was going to happen in her life. Even the end-of-the-summer school dance was exciting to my cousin. She wasn't the kind of girl who would run to the mall at the last minute to buy something to wear. I would tease her and tell her that some of the clothes she bought so early would be out of style by the time she wore them. But she didn't care what I said. She just always had to be prepared.

Everything had to match. The shoes, the bag, everything. Even her sunglasses. That was my cousin, all right! Always ready, down to her outfit and what time she would arrive. Never late for anything.

Jasmine enjoyed life and she enjoyed her family.

She enjoyed her friends and school. And now she's gone. At twenty-two years old, she is gone.

Gone forever.

I loved hanging out with Jasmine's college friends—the "honeys," as my friends at school call them. Life at North Carolina Central seemed like so much fun for them. I just wanted to be around the college kids as much as possible. I wanted to be a part of their lives. I spent all summer trying to hang out with them, and I definitely want to go to Central when I graduate from high school in two years. Going to NCCU is a family tradition. My grandpa and grandma were graduates from Central, and so were Aunt Shirley and Momma.

Jasmine made college look easy. She was the reason I was looking forward to college. She was just a happy person. Even when I wanted to cry, Jasmine would say something silly and make me laugh.

It was really hard to laugh when I came to live with Jasmine and my aunt and uncle, because nothing is easy when you're trying to deal with a drug-addicted momma. Daddy left to go back to Iraq at the end of my sophomore year two months ago. He pretty much ordered me to live with Aunt Shirley and Uncle Todd until he came back from the war. I had every intention of doing just that until my friends started telling me they'd seen Momma hanging out on the street corners again with some really bad people. To make matters worse, she was doing drugs and living with that no-good boyfriend, Bow.

After living in a homeless shelter last year and finally moving in with my cousin, I thought we were going to be safe. Momma had barely escaped going to jail after she fell asleep and burned down the homeless shelter. That's how we ended up at my aunt's house. But Momma went back into the hood to live with Bow, and I moved back too because I thought that was the only way to save her. Daddy was having none of that, and he was back in the States before I knew it. He hauled me back to my aunt Shirley and uncle Todd's house. I don't know if that was good or bad, because if I had stayed there with Momma, maybe I could have saved Jasmine from crazy Bow.

It's hard to believe that Jasmine's dead. It's hard to believe that I'll never be able to talk to her again. We talked all the time about everything. If I went back to Momma's for a few weeks, Jasmine would find a way to call me, even if my cell phone was turned off, which was usually the case. Most people thought that we were sister and brother, not first cousins. Not two sisters' children—sisters who have been paralyzed by pain all week.

I can't imagine how they feel. I just know that I'm hurting so bad. I feel like this is my fault. I wonder if Momma feels any guilt about how Jasmine died.

My moving back in with Aunt Shirley and Uncle Todd brought all of my troubles with me. I brought all of Momma's troubles to their house too. Problems I have been dealing with as the son of a drugged-out mother. The problems that I guess other teenagers have too when their daddies are away fighting a senseless war.

I miss my daddy and I'll be glad when he comes home. When he returns from Iraq this time, he won't have to go back. I'm counting the days from when he told me that he'd be home for good in six months. Daddy received a new assignment and he's still not back, but I'm excited knowing he'll be home forever this time. Maybe he can fix some of the madness in our lives. I wonder where we'll live. Maybe we'll move in with his girlfriend, Pauline, or stay here with my folks.

Yes, I brought all of that mess into my aunt and uncle's home, and now their baby is dead—dead from a bullet to the head.

The bullet came from Bow's gun. Bow's no good, and when he's caught, he'll go to jail where he belongs. I just don't believe God will leave things like this.

I know that Bow pulled the trigger, but I feel responsible for Jasmine's death. I feel like Momma killed her too. Maybe we both killed her with our problems.

I still wake up in the middle of the night thinking about how she died. I don't know how to explain it. There's a feeling of loneliness without Jasmine. A feeling that I'm the only person left on Earth. My chest hurts. My heart hurts. I just hurt all over.

CHAPTER TWO

All I know for sure is last Saturday morning changed all of our lives forever.

It's still like a bad dream. A dream I can't wake up from.

Jasmine and I were at home doing our Saturday-morning chores when Bow started banging on the mahogany and glass front door at Aunt Shirley's house.

Uncle Todd had told us to never answer the door when Bow came around. He had also told Bow to stop coming to his house trying to bully us. But Bow does as he pleases, when he pleases. He was trouble from the start. When he's not drinking, he's smoking; when he's not smoking, he's cursing. He always smells like marijuana or something illegal. He looks even worse than he smells. Bow is just bad, bad news. But you can't tell Momma that.

Momma smells and acts just like he does. No matter how much everyone warns Momma, she won't leave that fool alone. It's as if she has to have him in her life. I've always wondered what makes her so attractive to bad men and women. Momma's ex-sister-in-law, Aunt Clarine, is just as bad for Momma as Bow, but they are the two people Momma always wants to be around. She spends more time with them than she does with her own family, including me. My grandpa's dead now, but he always said, "Say what you want, but water will seek its own level."

It's taken losing Jasmine to get Bow off the streets and out of Momma's life. At least for now. I'll never forget the day Momma left Aunt Shirley's house with him. Just when I thought things were going to be okay, Uncle Todd caught them in the garage, where they had spent the night together. When Uncle Todd ran Bow off, Momma went with him. She just didn't seem to care what happened to me. I should've left things just the way they were, but no, I followed her back to Bow's house. Momma eventually left and moved in with Aunt Clarine, but she was still seeing Bow. He was always looking for her when they weren't together.

He was looking for Momma on the day he showed up at Aunt Shirley's house and destroyed our family.

"Open this damn door!" Bow yelled so that everyone on Walker Lane could hear him. He loved coming over and making a scene. He wanted the neighbors to know who he was and that he was as good as anybody else. He definitely wanted them to know that he was dating their neighbor's sister. Anything to make Uncle Todd look bad and to tick off Aunt Shirley.

Bow's favorite words are "I ain't no punk." Maybe he isn't a punk, but he sure is a junkie and now he's a murderer.

I refused to answer the door no matter how loud Bow knocked. That decision was the beginning of the worst day of my life. Oh God, I wish I had just let him in the house. Maybe if I'd opened the door, Bow wouldn't have gone crazy on us. Maybe I could've talked to him, talked him down. Maybe if I'd just opened the door, we wouldn't be in this church saying good-bye to my cousin and best friend in the whole world.

Jasmine was busy cleaning out the refrigerator when crazy Bow started his mess.

"Just ignore him," Jasmine said. Her voice was trembling.

Bow kicked the door several times. Then he hit it with a beer bottle and kicked it again, over and over. I heard glass shattering.

"Man, stop kicking that door!" I yelled from the kitchen as I tried to put the ramen noodles back in the pantry. Jasmine loved ramen noodles. Aunt Shirley could be cooking steaks, and that girl would still have made herself a bowl of noodles.

"Boy, tell your momma to come out here and bring me my money! Betty, get out here!" he yelled as loud as he could, and kicked the door again. This time he kicked the lock and we heard the door crack.

"I'm not telling my momma anything," I yelled as I walked toward the door. "Besides, she's not here!"

I looked at the crack in Aunt Shirley's expensive door and at all the broken glass.

"You'd better stop damaging this door, man. I'm telling you, Uncle Todd is not going to take your mess; and you just wait until I tell my daddy."

"Your daddy!? Boy, ain't nobody thinking about your G.I. Joe daddy. Betty! Betty, come out here now! You *know* you owe Big Daddy Bow some money."

"Man!" I yelled. "Get away from here before I call the police. I'm not playing with you."

"Playing with me? Boy, I am grown. I ain't playing. You want a toy, you'd better go and buy one."

Bang!!!

I just remember the blood. There was so much blood.

Jasmine was just walking in from the kitchen to see what was going on. That fool shot right through the stained glass in the door, through my cousin's head, and into the wall. The bullet went right past me and hit her. A bullet that was meant for me!

"Jasmine!" I yelled, and turned to my cousin. It was like watching a bad movie—a horror movie—in slow motion. I'll never forget the blank look on her face. No sound, no tears, just a look of shock. Her knees buckled as she crumpled to the floor like a rag doll.

"Damn!" I heard Bow yell as he ran off the porch and down the street.

I grabbed my cell phone and tried to call 911 with one hand while I was trying to hold my cousin's head together with the other. I couldn't get a signal. I was actually holding my cousin's head together with my hand. There was nothing I could do to help her. Nothing!

The doctor at Duke University Hospital said Jasmine probably never felt a thing, just shock. He said she was dead when she hit the living-room floor. In some kind of strange way, I'm grateful for that.

There was no screaming from Jasmine. Just a look in her beautiful, scared eyes that I'll never forget. Her blood shot across the room like it was water coming out of a toy water gun, landing all over Grandma and Granddaddy's wedding picture. The rest of her blood came running down her face, her neck, and all over her clothes and onto the floor.

The only thing worse than the blood were the screams that started to come from Aunt Shirley and Uncle Todd when they came home. They were on their way back from the grocery store when they drove past Bow running down the street. They knew something was wrong when they passed Bow, but they had no idea he had just murdered their only child. Only God knows how many people would have died if my aunt and uncle had arrived five minutes earlier. I think the only reason Bow didn't kill me is because he panicked and ran. I'm sure he didn't mean to leave the only witness alive.

Uncle Todd pushed open the busted door as he and Aunt Shirley came in with their grocery bags.

"Jasmine? Joseph? What in the world is going on? Did Bow kick in this door?" Uncle Todd asked, standing in the doorway.

Then he saw his baby. He saw the horrible sight of Jasmine lying there dead. I was still trying to dial 911, but my hands were shaking too badly to hold on to the cell phone.

"Oh Lord, my child!" Aunt Shirley shrieked. She dropped her grocery bags on the floor. An egg carton fell open, and the eggs broke just like my heart was breaking. Aunt Shirley grabbed her knees for a moment to try and hold herself up, but she couldn't stand. Her knees buckled like Jasmine's had and she fell to the floor, moaning.

"Jaaaaaaasssssmiiiiine!"

SHELIA P. MOSES

Aunt Shirley just lay down on the floor beside Jasmine and cried like I have never seen anyone cry. She got as close to Jasmine as she could get. She just kept kissing and hugging her lifeless body. It was like she was trying to breathe for Jasmine.

"Breathe, baby. Please breathe," she said in between tears. "Breathe, Jasmine, breathe," she said over and over again.

Uncle Todd stumbled to his knees and tried to put a couch pillow on the side of Jasmine's head to stop the bleeding. But it wouldn't stop. The blood was like a river draining the life out of our family. Jasmine not only died, she took a part of us with her.

"Call 911!" Uncle Todd screamed at me. "Dial 911, son!"

"I'm trying! I'm trying!"

Then I realized that my cell phone was dead.

It was as if everything stopped at the same time as Jasmine's heartbeat. Everything seemed to have frozen in time.

"Use the house phone, son, use the house phone," Uncle Todd said in between his own sobs.

"Stay with us, Jasmine. For God's sake, stay with us," Uncle Todd pleaded as he tried to do CPR on his baby girl.

I ran to Grandma's beautiful oak desk and dialed 911. I don't remember much of what the operator said except that our neighbor Mrs. Wilkins had already called, after hearing the gunshots, and that help was on the way.

I remember hanging up and running back to my aunt and uncle. Within minutes I could hear the sirens. Aunt Shirley's screams were louder than the sirens. Mrs. Wilkins ran into our house to try to help, but she knew it was useless.

"She's gone, Todd. Our baby is dead," Aunt Shirley said as she rolled around in the blood and broken eggs.

"Our baby is gone," she cried out.

Mrs. Wilkins started to pray. "'The Lord is my shepherd; I shall not want. / He maketh me to lie down in green pastures: . . .'"

"God help us," Uncle Todd said as he closed Jasmine's left eye. I hadn't noticed that Bow had actually shot her right eye out until Uncle Todd closed the one eye that remained.

I somehow found the strength to go over to the couch to get the colorful blanket that Jasmine had brought back for Aunt Shirley from her trip to Africa last summer. Jasmine was always going someplace nice. She said she wanted to see the world. Now it was over. She would never travel again. She would never do anything else with her young life.

I took the blanket and tried to cover Jasmine, but Aunt Shirley wouldn't let me.

"No, not my baby! Do not put that blanket over her head. She's afraid of the dark. Stop it!"

She didn't mean to, but Aunt Shirley pushed me down with one hand. I held Jasmine's blanket close to my chest as I stumbled to the floor. Mrs. Wilkins sat down beside me and tried to comfort me.

"'Yea, though I walk through the valley of the shadow of death, I will fear no evil,'" Mrs. Wilkins said.

Thank God the EMS people and the police arrived when they did. They pushed us all aside to attend to Jasmine as Aunt Shirley ran all over the living room calling for Grandma and Granddaddy like she thought they would come back to life and help us. Then she stopped and looked up at the ceiling. She was looking to the heavens.

"Is she with you, Momma? Please tell me that you can see my baby girl. Tell me that Jasmine is with you. You know she's afraid of the dark. Momma, she's afraid of the dark. Poppa, answer me. Tell me that you can see my baby. Momma, answer me." Aunt Shirley just kept on screaming like it was the end of the world, and maybe it was.

Then I somehow felt that Grandma and Granddaddy had come back from heaven or something. I swear that just for a second, for one brief second, Jasmine's body moved. No sign that she was still alive. Just a little jerk like she was moving on to the other world. I don't know for sure, but I believe she went to heaven with our grandparents at that very moment. She didn't move again.

Aunt Shirley looked at Grandma and Granddaddy's wedding picture, all covered in blood, and fainted. I was glad that she did, because Uncle Todd was out of control too as the EMS people prepared to take Jasmine's body away. He wasn't crying out loud like Auntie, he just moaned like a hurt animal or something.

When they lifted Jasmine's body up off the floor, a jar of jelly she had been holding in her hand fell and shattered.

Uncle Todd followed the EMS people to the door and out to the street.

"Is she dead? Is she dead?" he screamed over and over as other neighbors started to gather around outside. Uncle Todd followed them to the EMS van and tried to climb inside, but they told him it was best if we all followed in the car.

Mr. Wilkins, who had just driven up, volunteered to drive us in his car.

Uncle Todd came back in to get us and helped Aunt Shirley up from the bloody floor. My aunt woke up and started to moan even more when she realized that they'd taken Jasmine's body away.

I just sat there on the floor wrapped in the blanket that Mrs. Wilkins had put around me. I thought about how impossible all of this was. A police officer was asking me some questions, but I just couldn't answer them, and then Uncle Todd grabbed me up to take me to the hospital.

The officer said he would be back later to talk to us. In the car on the way to the hospital, I kept thinking about how scared Jasmine had been of crazy Bow and how she'd had every reason to be. He had terrorized her earlier in the summer when she came over to Momma's with my daddy, trying to get me to move out of that run-down place and back in with them.

Uncle Todd and Aunt Shirley had driven Daddy to the hood on the Southside to see me, but they didn't come inside Momma's apartment. Jasmine had insisted on coming in with Daddy, because no matter what happened, she had always been fond of Momma and she cared about me. Daddy and Momma were just sitting at the table talking when Bow came in raising hell about Daddy and Jasmine being in his house.

"Man, get up out of my house," Bow said as he took a drink of liquor straight out of the bottle.

Before I knew it, Daddy and Bow were fighting and Jasmine was screaming. She was so scared because Bow was threatening Daddy.

"The next time I see you, I'm gonna kill you!" Bow said as he threw the bottle against the wall. "I promise you that you are a walking dead man!"

I don't think a day passed all summer that Jasmine didn't mention how mean and evil Bow had looked when he said that to Daddy. It was almost as if she could see that something bad was going to happen.

She believed that Bow was capable of killing all of us.

But Daddy wasn't afraid of Bow.

"Kill me, Bow, but I'm not leaving here without my son," Daddy had shouted back. "I flew across the world to get him away from you. So kill me." Jasmine and I had never seen my daddy that mad before. Daddy was granted two weeks leave to come home. Who knows what he told his commanding officer so that he could come back to Durham.

Momma didn't put up much of a fight for me to stay with her. She just kept yelling at Daddy. "Joseph been living here for three weeks, and you need to give me some child support!"

Daddy totally ignored her and kept his eyes on crazy Bow as we left that house without one piece of my clothes. Jasmine and Daddy helped me move back in with my aunt and uncle, after we went shopping for new stuff.

I was so glad to get away from Momma and Bow, but now with all that's happened this week, there are days that I actually wish I'd stayed with Momma and Bow. Maybe Jasmine would still be alive. I wouldn't have been at her house, and crazy Bow wouldn't have come over. I don't know what to say to my aunt and uncle. They just keep hugging me and telling me that this wasn't my fault. Them saying it isn't my fault doesn't make me feel any better.

My aunt and uncle don't blame anybody. They just go on the best they can. I don't think they blame Momma, either. It's amazing to be here in this church and look at Momma sitting with the family like she doesn't know what happened. What's even more amazing is the fact they have welcomed her with open arms. Well, at least Aunt Shirley did. Uncle Todd keeps looking at Momma like he wants to murder her like Bow murdered his daughter.

When Jasmine was shot, I called Momma at Aunt Clarine's, where she was staying again. She came over to the hospital immediately and never left Aunt Shirley's side.

Aunt Shirley needed her sister so much, and I'm glad that Momma has been in some rehab long enough to keep herself together for at least a week.

That's what ticked Bow off. He didn't want Momma to get clean. He wanted her to stay in that dark hole with him. It's been a bad summer for Momma. She left Aunt Shirley's mad at all of us and moved in with Bow for a minute, but she left soon after Daddy made me move back to my aunt and uncle's house. Finally she went back to rehab, and it seemed like all was going pretty well. But there were still several problems. First, Momma was in the day program at rehab and staying with my bad-news Aunt Clarine again at night.

The other problem with Momma's rehab was that she was still sneaking around to see Bow.

Momma didn't know that Bow was looking for her last Saturday morning, because she had just gotten back from T.J. Maxx with Aunt Clarine. I could tell from her screaming that she hadn't heard the news. When Momma arrived at the hospital, she and Aunt Shirley just sat and looked at each other like they knew this kind of pain. They did. They knew death. They had buried their parents together. When the doctor pronounced Jasmine dead, the sisters wept as Uncle Todd and I sat beside them in shock.

Today Momma's sitting on one side of Aunt Shirley and Uncle Todd's sitting on the other side. They helped her walk into the church. I guess you can say they carried her in. She definitely couldn't walk in on her own. She seemed as lifeless as Jasmine.

CHAPTER THREE

I have never been to a funeral for a young person before.

You can tell from the crowd of people that Jasmine was loved. All of her teachers from elementary school, high school, and college are here. The women from her AKA sorority take up half the church, and they're all dressed in pink and green. My friend Valerie is here with her momma, Ms. Monet. Aunt Shirley asked them to sit with the family, and I feel good knowing Valerie is just two rows behind me.

Uncle Todd has a big family, and they've come from all over the country. It really makes me happy that my daddy's family drove over from Raleigh even though they weren't related to Jasmine. They came to support me because they knew Daddy couldn't get back from the war for the funeral.

Daddy's girlfriend, Pauline, is here looking beautiful as usual. I'm really glad to see her. Momma can say what she wants to about Pauline, but I wish Momma was more like her. Besides, Pauline is fine at forty-five. I love my momma, but she's too loud, she smokes too much, and she could care less about how she lives or how she affects others. But that Pauline is as fine as expensive sugar. She's a successful art gallery owner and is always trying to do something good for the community. Momma's always trying to do something for Momma. So I'm glad to see Miss Pauline sitting over there dressed in Chanel from head to toe. Ain't nothing wrong with that woman!

The only person you know doesn't belong here is Aunt Clarine. I'll never understand what my Uncle Ed saw in her to marry her and have a child with her. Their son, Ed Jr., is so embarrassed by the way she's dressed that he's refused to sit with her. Instead he's sitting with us, even though he wasn't related to Jasmine. Aunt Clarine has on the tightest dress she owns, with yellow shoes and a yellow bag. Who wears yellow shoes to a funeral? Not to mention, she brought her latest boyfriend, Ellsworth, with her.

For those who cannot see Aunt Clarine, they can definitely hear her screaming. One thing you can always depend on from Aunt Clarine, if she comes to a funeral, she's definitely going to show off.

Oh God. I was hoping they wouldn't open the casket again, but they're going to. That's the last thing that Aunt Shirley needs. The mortician,

Mr. Howard, is doing a good job, but we've cried enough. Why is he doing this?

One by one all the people in the church walk by Jasmine's coffin. She has so many friends and they're so sad. Aunt Clarine gets to the coffin and lets out this fake scream and faints. Old Ellsworth catches her as Ed Jr. hangs his head with shame.

The only people left to view the body now are our immediate family members. This is going to be hard.

Aunt Shirley and Uncle Todd walk like two people on death row heading to the electric chair. Momma and Uncle Todd hold Aunt Shirley up because she almost fell twice.

"My baby, my baby," Aunt Shirley whispers into Jasmine's ear. Uncle Todd's holding my aunt up with one arm and rubbing Jasmine's head slowly with his free hand. They had someone place a pretty pink head wrap on her, and you can't tell that the mortician rebuilt the right side of her head.

Momma says, "She's in a better place now, sister." I'm expecting Aunt Shirley to turn around and slap my momma. Instead she hugs Momma and they cry together.

Uncle Todd looks at Momma like he wants to say, "Well, if it's so much better, why aren't you dead instead of Jasmine?" But he doesn't say anything while he watches the sisters cry. They cry like they did when Grandma and Granddaddy died. Uncle Todd looks over Aunt Shirley's black hat with the netting and practically rolls his eyes at Momma again. He's really looking at her like he wants her to be in that casket, not his baby. Not his one and only child, who was never in trouble a single day in her short life. The child who was destined for greatness.

Mr. Howard closes the casket and it's over. When

he closes the casket, Aunt Shirley's head falls back like her neck is broken. She screams, "Oh, I will never see my child's face again!"

None of us will ever see Jasmine again.

After the service we take the long, sad ride to Oak Cemetery to say our final good-byes. The limousines head up the hillside to where Granddaddy and Grandma are buried side by side. It's raining so hard now that you can barely see the tent where we're getting ready to leave Jasmine.

Burials are sad, but there's something nice about watching the AKA sisters walk across the cemetery making their signature sound—the AKA make a sound like little birds calling for a missing baby bird, a baby bird named Jasmine. The rain's not stopping them. They're marching like soldiers coming to bury their own.

When Mr. Howard instructs the family to leave, the sorority sisters remain behind at Jasmine's grave. We can still hear the little bird sounds as Momma, my aunt and uncle, and I drive away together in the limo.

Aunt Shirley cries all the way home. "Todd, please, we cannot leave our baby, please." We all start to cry again.

It seems like everyone in Durham comes to the repast at the house. The lawyers and staff from Aunt Shirley's firm are here, and all of Uncle Todd's golf buddies and every airline pilot who's not flying today have made their way here too. My friends from school and my old neighbors have been stopping by all week. Valerie's been over to the house almost every day with Ms. Monet.

I think it's safe to say Valerie and I are dating now.

We've been working at Target together all summer and we kissed once. A short kiss. I like her a lot.

I don't think Ms. Monet would let us date if I was still living with Momma. She just doesn't understand why Momma is the way she is, and she doesn't want Valerie around Momma for too long. Before I moved to Aunt Shirley's, I only saw Valerie in passing and wished I could've had a girl like her for my girlfriend.

It would be a respectable repast if Aunt Clarine had not shown up and shown off. It wasn't enough to cry the loudest at the funeral; she has to talk the loudest at the repast. What makes her think she is welcome here is a mystery to everyone. No matter what's going on in the family, she just shows up uninvited and unannounced. She's been divorced from my uncle for a long time, and we would've forgotten her by now, but she keeps popping up, and most often with Momma. Uncle Ed might've been smart enough to move to Alaska to get away from her, but Aunt Clarine's smart enough to show up the minute she hears he's in town for the funeral. Her favorite words are "I can go anyplace my son can go. We are a package deal." Lord, I wouldn't want to be the one having to open that package every time there's a family event.

Like Daddy's other siblings, Uncle Ed knew Daddy couldn't be here, so he and Ed Jr. came all the way down from Alaska to see how I was doing. My uncle is a good man, and I wish he and Ed Jr. could stay longer so I could get to know them better.

But they can see that no one's going to throw Aunt Clarine out, so they'll leave soon for sure. The person throwing Aunt Clarine out is usually Aunt Shirley, but she doesn't have the strength today. So Aunt Clarine is free to roam around and make a complete fool of herself. I don't think she's noticed that the only person in the room talking to her is Momma. Uncle Ed is on his third glass of wine as she turns to him again, trying to talk about what is going on with Ed Jr.

"So, I bet our boy's making all A's out there in that cold place," Aunt Clarine says to my uncle.

"Excuse me, but I have to go to the restroom," Uncle Ed says, and he almost runs away from his ex.

Oh Lord . . . here she comes.

"Hey, Joseph, where's your daddy?" Aunt Clarine asks like she really cares. She can't harass Uncle Ed, so now it's my turn to listen to her. Ed Jr. already went upstairs to lie down, pretending to have a headache to get away from his own mother.

At the end of the day, Aunt Clarine doesn't care about Daddy or Momma. She cares about herself and creating drama, just like Momma.

As much pain as Aunt Shirley's in, she isn't going to tolerate Clarine another minute.

"Put that cigarette out in my house," Aunt Shirley says as Clarine lights up a Marlboro Light.

"Sorry, girl. I forget you uptown black folks don't smoke. I just want to let you know how much I loved Jasmine." She takes one long puff before putting her cigarette out in one of Aunt Shirley's flowerpots. Momma can see all the drama happening from across the room, and she runs over.

"Sister, why don't you take Clarine outside for some fresh air," Aunt Shirley says to Momma as she walks away from Aunt Clarine.

"Yes, that's a good idea," Momma says as she looks at Aunt Shirley with so much sadness. She knows she's wrong for letting Aunt Clarine even come into the house. Momma seems to be getting tired of Clarine, but not fast enough for the rest of us. Why is she here? That dress is just too small and her legs are a mess, but I'm still trying to get past the yellow shoes.

Not to mention, Ellsworth is walking around behind Aunt Shirley looking like he's her manager for one of those reality TV shows. He knows he's wrong for wearing those ugly matching orange pants and shirt to the funeral. Poor guy, he has no idea why he's even here. Aunt Clarine's just trying to make Uncle Ed mad. I can honestly tell her that Uncle Ed could care less if she brought the pope to these family functions. What my uncle really wants is for her to stay home with her folks and leave him and Ed Jr. alone. She just has this baby mama drama thing going that is unreal.

"That Shirley is so uppity!" Aunt Clarine says as she walks away from me and Valerie.

"Be quiet," Momma says to Aunt Clarine loud enough for half the people in the room to hear.

Okay! Now I am really embarrassed. Well, I thought I was embarrassed. Nothing is as embarrassing as Ellsworth running behind Aunt Clarine with a chicken bone hanging out of his mouth.

Valerie doesn't even see Mr. Chicken Bone because she's so busy watching Aunt Clarine being rushed out the door by Momma.

"Who is that?" Valerie asks, shaking her head.

"You don't want to know," I answer as we eat some of the catered food that the law firm has sent over.

"She looks a hot mess," Valerie says as she looks over at Aunt Clarine again. "Are you going to stay here with your uncle and aunt, Joseph?" Valerie asks, trying to ignore Aunt Clarine lighting up another cigarette at the door.

"Yes," a voice from behind us says. It's Uncle Todd. I look at his swollen eyes and I want to cry again, but I'm trying to be strong.

"Yes, he is staying here. Joseph, don't even think about leaving. This is your home, and I promised your dad that I would take care of you until he comes back."

I don't say anything because I know how upset daddy would be if I left again.

"Daddy was very sad when I told him about Jasmine. He tried to get leave, but the army wouldn't let him," I say to Uncle Todd.

"I know he did, son. I've talked to him several times this week. Having you here is more than enough. And it was really nice for your family to come. Your daddy will be home for good in just a few months. Now, get some food in you to keep your strength up. And then you can help me start saying good-bye to our visitors. It's been a long day."

Uncle Todd walks away with his head down. He didn't say anything to Valerie and hardly looked at her. I think she just reminds him too much of Jasmine. They really do look alike, with their neatly cut bob haircuts and their love for Gap clothes.

Jasmine liked Valerie and called her "little twin." Most of all, she liked Valerie for me. She wanted her to be my girlfriend more than I did.

"Find yourself a nice girl, cousin. A girl like Valerie. Don't date just anybody." She would laugh when she said that, but she meant it from the bottom of her heart.

Now I have only one cousin, Ed Jr., and I rarely see him.

"Take care, cousin," he says to me as he and Uncle Ed get ready to leave with the rest of my family.

"Thanks for coming, man," I say to my cousin, giving him a big hug.

Soon the visitors are gone, including Valerie and Ms. Monet, and Momma is back inside the house, smelling like smoke, of course. Everything is still, except the clock on the wall is ticking so loud.

Momma doesn't seem too comfortable now that everything is quiet.

"Well, sister, I understand if you want me to leave," Momma says to Aunt Shirley. "I'll check on you tomorrow."

Aunt Shirley looks over at Uncle Todd as if she's a little girl again. She knows that Uncle Todd doesn't want Momma here, but it seems like Aunt Shirley has gotten amnesia since Jasmine died. She's forgotten all the bad things that Momma did to her. The bad things Momma did to all of us, mainly bringing that drug dealer Bow over here in the first place. She's forgotten that Jasmine's dead because of Momma's bad choices.

"Stay as long as you like," Uncle Todd says as he walks into the kitchen to make Aunt Shirley some tea.

That's what his mouth says.

His eyes say, *Get your sorry behind out of my house.*

Momma and Aunt Shirley just sit on the couch in the living room, where Jasmine died, like two old women waiting on the Lord. I sit in the chair in front of them, not knowing what to do. The sisters are looking at Grandma and Granddaddy's picture. I wiped the blood off the glass, but now it seems to be covered with tears.

They're sitting there like they're waiting for Jasmine to walk back in the door.

CHAPTER FOUR

Two weeks have passed and all is quiet at the house
until Momma announces during our Saturday
dinner that she's going back to the apartment complex in Southside—to the run-down complex where
she was staying with Bow before she went to rehab
and to live with Aunt Clarine.

"I'm moving back to Henry Homes today,"
Momma says like she's going to the store for ice cream.

I'm so mad. Jasmine's been dead for only two
weeks and Aunt Shirley really needs us all. Momma

should stay a little longer. She's too selfish to realize that she's needed here. Even with all of her sister's problems, Aunt Shirley seems to be clinging to Momma the most, sometimes even more than to Uncle Todd.

But no, Momma is ready to go. Ready to go back to the land of trouble. Uncle Todd looks relieved that she is leaving, but Aunt Shirley looks sad. She knows that it'll only take one vial of crack cocaine for Momma to be on the streets again. One drink and she'll be in a shelter again. Worst of all, she could meet up with Bow again or someone just like him. One thing I realize is that Bow could've been any old Joe Blow on the street. There's nothing special about him that Momma loves. She just likes a guy that's no good, with drugs to sell or give to her. Nope, there is nothing special about Bow; he is just Momma's kind of no-good guy.

"Stay here, sister," Aunt Shirley begs.

"I'll be back. I promise. Besides, I'm just moving twenty-five minutes away. It's time for me and Joseph to go home."

"Joseph?" Aunt Shirley pushes her plate away. She was only picking at the food anyway.

"You can leave whenever you feel like, but the boy stays here," Uncle Todd says firmly, without even looking up from his plate of food that he was not eating.

"No, it's time for us to leave and give you all some privacy," Momma says.

I'm thinking, *Who is "us"?*

Uncle Todd slams his hand down on the table, rattling the dishes and making us all jump.

"Privacy! I do not want privacy, Betty! I want my child back. Can you find that sorry man of yours and turn back the hands of time? Can you do that?"

"No, I can't," Momma says loudly. "And you can't replace Jasmine with Joseph. He's my son and he's not staying here. Let's go, Joseph." She pushes back from the table.

"Momma!" I can't believe she's saying those words.

"How can you bring up Jasmine at a time like this?" Aunt Shirley says in total disbelief. "Get out of my house, girl. You come in here like you're sorry, with your same old bull. My daughter is dead because you showed that crackhead where we lived. Now you want to take Joseph? I'll have to be as dead as Jasmine before I let you take my nephew out of here! Now get your sorry behind out of my house."

"Joseph's sixteen now. He can decide for himself." Momma looks over at me. "What do you want to do, son?"

Does she really believe I want to go back to that hole in the wall and live with her again?

I look at Momma and I look at my aunt and uncle. My eyes stray over to the new carpet on the living-room floor—carpet they had to replace because Jasmine's blood ruined the other one. For a moment I think I see her body lying there.

"Momma, I can't leave Aunt Shirley. She needs me more than ever," I say as I continue to look at the new carpet.

Momma just looks at me like I've done something horrible to her.

"Doesn't matter what I need. You are not leaving this house, Joseph!" Aunt Shirley shouts as she looks at Momma.

Momma storms away from the table. "You never change, boy. You just like your daddy and his uppity folks."

I follow Momma into the living room and notice Momma's bags sitting next to the new front door.

As usual, Momma had already planned to leave long before she said a word to anyone. I walk outside behind her and stand on the porch.

This is the story of my life, I'm thinking as Momma walks out of my life again. She's dragging her suitcase like a college girl going to her dorm.

I don't know why, but I think about the time Momma got into an argument with Aunt Shirley when I was about six years old. I heard Aunt Shirley tell Momma that she wasn't being a good mother to me while Daddy was away working for the airline in New York for six months.

Momma didn't even try to defend herself. She looked at Aunt Shirley and said, "Are you calling me a bad mother?"

"Yes," Aunt Shirley said very matter-of-factly.

"Well, you keep him, then. You keep Joseph if you think you can do a better job."

And Momma just walked away. I didn't see her again until Daddy came back to get me months later.

Momma was always leaving me with somebody, and now she talks like she's been the best mother in the world. Maybe Momma doesn't realize that I actually remember her running in and out of my life. I don't think she understands that I remember all the things she used to do, like stealing the silverware at restaurants and changing the price tags in the stores when we went shopping. It's all a blank to her now, but it's not to me. She honestly believes that I don't remember when I was in the fourth grade and she was beating me in front of the school with a belt because I was dirty from playing outside. Aunt Shirley was on the school board and just happened to be coming to the school for a meeting and saw Momma hitting me. She pulled me away from Momma and told her to never hit me again. Aunt Shirley dropped Momma off at the train station with no protest from Momma. I don't know where Momma went that day, but Aunt Shirley took me home with her. You'd think Momma would've cared that Aunt Shirley was taking me away, but she really didn't.

I remember all of Momma's different boyfriends and the many times that we moved after she ran Daddy away. In between moves she was always leaving me with someone . . . anyone. Sometimes she would leave me for days with people I barely knew. If you listen to Momma now, you'd think she was the best momma in the world.

I used to cry when Momma would leave me, but not today.

I'm going to let her go.

I'm going to let her go for Jasmine.

I'm going to let her go for Aunt Shirley and for Uncle Todd.

I'm going to let her go for my daddy.

I'm going to let her go because I have to, for my own life.

I walk back inside to look for Aunt Shirley and Uncle Todd. Uncle Todd's on the telephone, probably leaving Daddy a voice mail to fill him in on Momma's latest move. I walk all over the house looking for Aunt Shirley, but she's not downstairs. I go upstairs and find her sitting in Jasmine's room holding her comforter in her arms.

"This room still smells like her, Joseph." She pulls the comforter close like it's Jasmine as she rocks back and forth. "Sometimes, son, I feel like I'm going to roll up in a big ball and just die," my aunt sobs.

"I know, Auntie. It feels like she's all over this house."

We're not ready to forget her smell. We're not ready to forget her. We can't.

I sit with my aunt in Jasmine's room most of the night. Finally she curls up in Jasmine's bed, still holding the comforter tight, and falls asleep. I lie on the floor so I can keep an eye on my aunt. I look under the bed and see Jasmine's small shoes all lined up just the way she left them.

My organized cousin. I find myself smiling. It feels good to smile.

Uncle Todd comes into the room in the middle of the night and lies down beside Aunt Shirley. I pretend I'm asleep. I listen to them cry together.

I cry too.

They eventually cry themselves to sleep.

I'm going to miss my Jasmine. I get up to use her laptop, which is still sitting on her desk in the little room connected to her bedroom. I'm looking online at all the classes I'm planning to take in the fall. All the classes Jasmine helped me select. She was excited for me. She even helped me pick out new clothes with money Daddy sent me. Money that he told me not to tell Momma I had. She was always taking my money and using it for drugs or to go clubbing.

It's been a few days since I've written my dad, so I send him an e-mail.

Hey, Dad!

I miss you!

I know I don't have to tell you how sad this house is. I know I don't need to tell you how sad Aunt Shirley and Uncle Todd are. We all miss Jasmine. It's hard to believe she's never coming back to us.

I know you're going to find this out, so I

might as well tell you now. Momma moved out
again, but I didn't go with her.

Daddy, do you think she's using drugs
again? I hope not.

At least I know you're coming back. Come
back soon, Daddy.

Your son,

Joseph

I can't fight the tears as I lie back on the floor
in Jasmine's room. I just want to be near my uncle
and aunt. I'm just glad they're finally sleeping a little.
When Jasmine first died, they stayed up for days.
They'd just walk the floor until two and three in the
morning. When they got tired of walking, they'd go
into the kitchen and drink coffee for the rest of the
night.

Sometimes I could hear them crying late at night.

When I wake up, Aunt Shirley and Uncle Todd have both left Jasmine's bedroom. I just lie there a minute and think about all the nights I slept in here on the floor so that Jasmine and I could talk. Sometimes Uncle Todd would make me go to my room because they were sick of listening to us laugh.

Jasmine talked to me almost every day about getting ready for school in the fall. She was so excited that I was living with them again.

On Monday morning I get ready to go to my summer job at Target. This is my last week at work before school starts. At breakfast no one says a word about Momma. I kiss Aunt Shirley and say good-bye to Uncle Todd as I run out to catch the bus.

When the bus stops in front of the store, I can barely get up out of my seat. I realize that this is the first day I've been away from my family since Jasmine died.

My coworkers are really glad to see me, and they all tell me how sorry they are for my family's loss. I try not to think about Jasmine as I put my Target name tag on my red shirt.

Jasmine was always stopping by the store to say hello and to have lunch with me. My cousin loved a good sub sandwich with everything on it, and so do I. She worked across the street at the Gap to secure her discount for her favorite clothes. Next to the Gap, she loved shopping at Target. She was a girl who would make a Target top look like it came from Neiman Marcus.

Jasmine loved the fact that I stocked food in the grocery department, because I got a discount too. She used it a lot more than I did.

"Joseph, please come to the front of the store,"

a voice suddenly says over the intercom.

Am I dreaming? I have to remind myself that Jasmine's dead and she can't be in the store today.

I take my gloves off and go to the front center aisle. I'm shocked to see Momma here as I get closer to the entrance. She usually sleeps late because she's not working. Again.

"Momma, what are you doing here?" I ask as I walk over to her.

"I just want to see how you're doing. I know you're upset about the other day. I'm sorry I stormed out like that." Momma says it all like she's really sincere. "Are you okay?" she asks.

"I'm fine, Momma, but I can't talk right now. I'm working. I need to unpack some boxes. You know today is my first day back at work."

"I just want to see you, baby. I don't want them to take you away from me."

"Them? Them *who*, Momma? They're our family. No one wants to hurt us. They're trying to help us. Why can't you see that?"

"No, they're *your* family. They love you, not me."

"What's wrong with you?" I ask her as if I don't know. Her eyes are looking in my direction, but not at me. I can always look in her face and tell when she's been up all night or doing drugs early in the morning. I guess I've been so preoccupied with Jasmine's death, I didn't notice Momma much at the house. Her face is sunken in and kind of dark, and I notice now that she's smaller than I have seen her in a long time. But it's the crazy look in her eyes that scares me the most. Two nights away from us and she is totally cracked out again. So much for rehab!

"Momma, no one is taking me away from you. Please, I have to get back to work."

"All right, all right," she says as I start to walk away. "Joseph!"

"Yes, Momma." I stop but don't turn around.

"I need bus fare to get home."

Unbelievable. She's just unbelievable. I build up enough nerve to turn around and look at her. In two days she has smoked up all the money that she has in the world. Just two short days.

"Dude, you got a job, I don't," she says, like I'm really the father and she's my kid. "I'm the one that got you this far in life. I'm about business. I'm the one that raised you. Not your aunt and uncle and not your daddy. Me!"

I don't say anything. I just reach into my pocket and give her ten dollars so that she'll leave my job. Ten dollars that was supposed to be for my lunch and bus fare to get home. I don't want to waste time getting change, so I walk away quickly, hoping that no one saw me giving her money. Of course I could never be that lucky. Valerie walks in as Momma is leaving.

"Hi, Ms. Betty," Valerie says politely as she looks at the money in Momma's hand.

"Hey, Valerie. My boy is such a good dude. He just gave me ten bucks. Can't nobody tell me that he's not going to the pros and buy me a big old house one day. Chicago Bulls, here he comes."

I don't have the words to express how I feel right now.

Valerie tries to ignore her, but Momma won't let you ignore her. Ignoring Momma only causes her to get louder and act crazier than you can imagine.

"Do you do nice things for your mother?" Momma asks Valerie, like she's really asking her a question that a mother should ask a child.

"Yes, I try," Valerie answers, with deep hurt on her face for me.

"See you later, Momma," I say as I try to get away from her before she embarrasses me even more.

But now she has enough money for some crack and bus fare, and I'm the furthest thing from her mind as she walks away.

Valerie has to clock in, so she doesn't have time to talk to me about Momma, and I'm so glad.

The rest of the day I keep thinking about Momma showing up at my job and embarrassing me. I think about Jasmine and how supportive she would have been if I'd told her what Momma did.

More and more I know that Momma's never going to get any better. Just for a minute I thought she was going to get herself together and come home to us. I don't mean just moving in for good; I mean that my old momma would come back. The momma I remember from when I was a little boy. A very little boy! Before Momma ever picked up a joint or a rock of crack cocaine. The one who used to read to me until I would fall asleep. She would cook the best pancakes in the whole world. I want her back.

I try to avoid Valerie for the rest of the day. I can't get Momma off of my mind, but I don't want to talk about her. No need to try to explain Momma every day of my life. There's little to explain, and people can see for themselves that she has a whole mess of problems.

Uncle Todd's sitting in his car in the parking lot waiting for me when I get off work. Valerie left work early, so I couldn't ride home with her.

"Hey, Uncle. You didn't have to pick me up. I'm happy to catch the bus." I'm not about to tell him that I was planning to walk home after I gave Momma all my money.

"No, son, the streets are no place for you after dark. I want to make sure you get home safely."

We don't talk much after that. He's been staying close to me around the house ever since Jasmine died. I think Uncle Todd's afraid that Bow will come after me so that I can't testify against him.

I don't think about Bow as much as I probably should. I know I'll have to testify against him. I just think of the pain that he's caused us. I know they'll catch him and he'll be behind bars and the law will make him pay for what he did to Jasmine. There's a $20,000 reward for Bow, and Uncle Todd says hundreds of tips have already come in to the police. When they catch Bow, I owe it to my cousin to go into the courtroom and tell the truth.

Momma swears that she hasn't heard from Bow, and I pray that she's telling the truth. I would hate to think that she would ever have anything else to do with that man. But I know Momma will do any-thing for drugs, and if Bow's hanging around with some crack, she'd be the first in line.

I work all week, and Aunt Shirley and Uncle Todd try to get back into a normal routine, but that's hard. Everything's hard without Jasmine.

CHAPTER FIVE

The following Monday is a terrible day for all of us.

It's the first day of school after being out all summer. Jasmine was supposed to drive me to school in her Volkswagen. It's hard getting up and walking out that door without her. That girl wanted to show off her new rims. She was miss prissy, but she loved cars like a guy. I always thought that was pretty funny.

Next week would've been the start of graduate school for Jasmine. I was really looking forward to helping her get settled in at Central and hanging out with her girlfriends again. But my cousin is gone and now her car is sitting in the garage with dust on it beside her bike that she loved to ride so much.

No one says much at breakfast.

"Need a ride, man?" Uncle Todd asks me as he looks over at Aunt Shirley to make sure she is okay.

I think Aunt Shirley needs him more than I do this morning.

"No, Uncle, I'll catch the bus."

I excuse myself from the table and grab my book bag and tennis racket so that I can make it to the bus stop on time.

I haven't seen some of my classmates all summer, but many came to the funeral. My friends Nick and Paul are waiting for me at the front door of the school when the bus drops me off at Dulles High. They're waiting so that they can walk with me to class. I saw them briefly at the funeral and the repast, but they kind of left me alone to spend time with my family and Valerie.

It's harder than I thought it would be walking down the hallways with people asking me how I'm doing and how Aunt Shirley and Uncle Todd are doing. I wonder if Momma has any idea what she's done to us. I wonder if she really understands what she did when she brought Bow into our lives.

"Hi, Joseph. Did you have a good summer?" Coach Williams asks as he passes my friends and me in the hallway. I stop to talk to my tennis coach, but nothing comes out of my mouth. I want to tell him that I was doing fine until Momma's boyfriend came over and blew my cousin's head half off. But I just can't talk. I try, but tears come out of my eyes instead of words coming out of my mouth.

Coach has been in New York all summer and got back just in time for classes to start. He doesn't know about Jasmine. Paul starts to explain what happened as he tries not to cry himself. Everyone is touched by my loss. Everyone is touched by such a horrible end to summer.

"Son, it'll be all right. You have to try to get past this as much as you can. Jasmine was a fine girl and her life can't be in vain." Coach knew Jasmine very well from her days at Dulles High. Like everyone else, he liked Jasmine.

Coach's words are with me all day as I somehow manage to get from class to class without falling apart.

I run into Valerie a couple of times in the hallway and I see her crying as she walks away.

When I get home from school, Aunt Shirley's sitting on the back porch. She's just sitting there, staring and still. Uncle Todd's mowing the grass for the second time in a week. Both of them are either cleaning or sleeping these days.

"Joseph, your daddy called!" Uncle Todd yells from the backyard.

"What did Daddy say?" I ask Aunt Shirley as I lean down to kiss her tear-streaked cheek.

"He was just checking on us, and he sent you a letter. It's on your bed." She pauses for a moment. "Your dad wants to make absolutely sure you're not staying with your mother. She's just no good for you right now, son."

"Figures." It makes me mad to hear Aunt Shirley say that. No matter how bad Momma can be, it still hurts to hear other people talk badly about her, even Momma's sister.

"Stop that mess, boy. Your daddy loves you, and my sister loves herself. Now, go do your homework. Dinner will be ready soon."

I don't want to upset Aunt Shirley any more. She's never looked so bad in all the years that I have known her. She just sits on that porch like she's waiting for Jasmine to come home from class. It's amazing how one summer, or even one day, can change your life forever.

"Okay, Auntie," I say as I touch my aunt lightly on the shoulder, then go upstairs. I read my letter from Daddy as soon as I get to my room.

Hello, Son,

How are you? I'm doing fine, but I miss my boy.

I got your e-mail and I was really glad to hear from you.

How's school? I know you will make good grades this year!!!

Enjoy tennis, but your grades always come

first. Remember that Arthur Ashe was the world's greatest, but he was also very well educated and well read.

Looks like I might be coming home sooner than later. It will definitely be before the six months I thought I would have to serve. I will keep you posted.

Daddy loves you.

I put my letter in the shoe box under my bed with all the other letters Daddy has written over the years and go downstairs to have dinner with my folks.

I miss my cousin every single day, but when it's time to sit down and eat, it gets even harder.

"The salmon's really good," I say to Aunt Shirley, trying to make small talk.

She barely takes her eyes off the chair that Jasmine usually sits in. "Thank you, Joseph. I'm glad you like it. Do you have homework on your first day back at school?"

"Yes, I do. I'll get started right after dinner."

Aunt Shirley is so wonderful. Her daughter is dead and she still finds the heart to care about other people's children.

She still cares about me.

"Do you think you'll play tennis again this year?" Aunt Shirley asks as she picks at her food almost as much as Uncle Todd is picking at his.

"Of course he will," Uncle Todd answers for me.

Those are the first words he has spoken to me since he told me that Daddy called. I've started to notice that he talks less and less each day. He seems to be in another world most of the time.

"I plan to try out for the team again. Coach said I can start tomorrow. He's been gone for the summer, but the assistant coach handled the tryouts that I missed."

"That's good news, son," Uncle Todd says with a slight smile.

I finish my dinner and go upstairs to do my homework. I don't know if I'll ever adjust to sitting at that table without Jasmine. Dinnertime was always saved for each of us to talk about our day. We talked about how much progress we'd each made on our tasks, and our highs and lows. Jasmine always had the most to say. She always had the most to tell us about her wonderful day.

I skip watching TV and go to bed as soon as I finish my homework. I close my eyes and try to get some sleep.

My cell phone rings early the next morning.

"Hey, it's me! Wake up. It's your momma."

"What's wrong, Momma?"

"Nothing's wrong. I just need to borrow twenty dollars for gas money."

"Gas money? You don't have a car."

"Do not question me, boy. Do you have twenty dollars or not?"

"Are you doing drugs again, Momma?"

She hangs up without answering me, but that's my answer. She just can't hold it together. No matter how hard she tries. But I really don't think she tries that hard.

I get dressed and run downstairs for breakfast and to catch a ride with Uncle Todd. When he's not on pilot duty, he always plays golf early in the morning, and the course is a mile from my school. Uncle Todd drops me off at school, and I try to rush right into the building, but it's too late. Momma's waiting for me in front of the principal's office. She knows better than to let Uncle Todd see her. I knew she would be here. I just knew it.

"Who you back-talking, boy?" she yells.

Oh, she's definitely back on drugs. I rush over to her so that no one else will hear her making a fool out of herself and me.

"Momma, what are you doing here? Why are you talking so loud?"

"Loud! You haven't heard loud. I'm your mother and I just wanted to borrow twenty dollars. Why can't you help a sister out?"

I reach into my pocket and give her a twenty-dollar bill and walk away. The only money I have until next payday.

Without even saying thank you, Momma leaves. "Later, dude," she says instead.

My job at Target is fast becoming a waste of time, because every dime I earn I have to give to Momma. Daddy would die if he knew I was giving her my money. Again!

CHAPTER SIX

After first period I rush to the gym to register for tennis. Up until Jasmine died, I was practicing all summer with the guys at the YMCA preparing for tryouts. I know I'm ready for the team. I missed the initial tryouts because of Jasmine's death, but Coach is giving me makeup tryouts. My grandma used to say, "God is a second-chance God. Even for small things." So here's my chance.

"Good to see you back in the gym," Coach says as he's walking in and I'm walking out.

"It's good to be back, Coach," I say as I rush to study period.

I'm in my seat for a few minutes when Paul comes in and sits down next to me.

"Hey, man, what's up with your momma? She just joning you today?"

"Mind your business, man." I just put my head down and pretend I'm studying. It's hard trying to go to school and deal with Momma at the same time. It's hard to defend Momma because she's always making a fool out of herself and me.

I thought things would change after Jasmine died, but I think Momma and Clarine will always be the way they are. They're so miserable and they do everything in their power to make other people miserable.

Finally the last period bell rings and I can go out to the tennis courts. Tennis is really cool this year because we have an outdoor and an indoor court. I practice hard with the other team members and try not to think about Jasmine. If she were alive, she'd be cheering very quietly for me.

"Go, Joseph!" I hear a voice coming from the stands.

"Jasmine?" I swing at the ball and miss.

I look up in the stands and see Momma. She's back at the school, and that means she's already spent the twenty dollars I gave her on crack. She's back for more. I don't have any more money and I don't know what to do now.

"Go, Joseph!" she screams again as I try to ignore her. The more I ignore her, the louder she gets. Other parents are looking at her now. What's normally a very quiet place is becoming Momma's theater. I finally wave so that she'll lower her voice.

After practice I walk toward the gym showers

only to find Momma waiting for me at the door.

"Joseph, I can't believe that you've been working all summer and you don't want to look out for me. Can't you see that Momma got it bad? Momma got it real bad."

I hug her tight and whisper in her ear, "Momma, please don't embarrass me, please."

I don't even take a shower. I just lead Momma away from the door and away from my tennis mates.

I look up and I see Uncle Todd walking toward us.

Thank you, God.

"Hi, Betty," he says as he tries not to look at Momma.

"Hey, brother, what you know good?"

"Don't 'brother' me. Why are you here in this school dressed like that? Do you ever think about your son?"

I was so busy trying to get her away from my

teammates that I didn't even notice she's wearing a short skirt that's way too tight and a midriff top.

"Oh, Momma," I say in disbelief as I look at her clothes.

"Don't 'Momma' me, boy. I wear what I wanna wear. I am your momma; you're not my daddy."

I never talk back to Momma, but I want to say, "You could fool me!" I could not dare say that. Granddaddy always said, "Follow God, not man. Learn your Bible." The Bible says to honor your mother and father, and I try to do that in spite of Momma's ways.

"Let's get out of here," Uncle Todd says as he pulls me away from Momma.

"What about me?" Momma whines to Uncle Todd, as if he really cares how she's going to get home.

I'm so hurt for her. To come to school dressed like that, I know she's back on drugs.

"Let's give her a ride, Uncle Todd," I say quietly.

He barely looks at Momma but says, "Where do you live now, Betty?"

"Same place, man."

"Where is 'same place'?" Uncle Todd says in his *I am sick of you!* voice. As if he has forgotten that Momma is back at Henry Homes.

"Over on King Road in Henry Homes," Momma says with pride.

King Road is one of the worst streets in Durham. Why would she want to live there again when all she has to do is straighten up her act and move back in with us?

When we drive up to the front entrance of the run-down apartments, I can't hold back my tears. I'd forgotten how bad it was living in this neighborhood. I think Uncle Todd actually feels a little sorry for Momma too. He doesn't say much, he just opens the door to get her out of his car as fast as possible.

"I'll be right back," I say, getting out to walk my momma to the door.

"Why do you want to live like this, Momma? Why don't you come home with us?"

"Boy, they don't want me over there. They blame me for Jasmine's death, and you do too."

I don't say anything. What can I say?

"Bye, Momma. I love you," I say. And I hug her tight.

"Love you, too," she whispers in my ear.

I turn and walk away.

"Oh, the reason I stopped by your scho—"

"I don't have any money, Momma." I cut Momma off and don't even turn around.

"Right," she says as she slams the door.

Uncle Todd is silent when I get back in the car.

When we pull into our driveway, he turns off the motor and looks at me.

"Son, you have to save yourself from Betty."

"That's my momma. I can't just stop loving her. I know you can, but she's my blood."

"You don't have to stop loving her, son, but you have to save *yourself*. You have to cut her off until she agrees to get some help. This in and out of drug rehab isn't working. The day retreat isn't working. She needs to be committed to a full-time live-in rehabilitation center. Your aunt and I have looked into a place in Raleigh. If Betty doesn't agree to go, we want you to stop seeing her and we'll have her banned from your school grounds."

I'm not going to say anything because I know it won't take much for the school administrator to ask Momma to never come back to that campus again. The teachers don't care for Momma at all, and they all start walking in the other direction when they see her coming. They would rather call Daddy in Iraq about me and my classes before they call Momma. Of course, Momma doesn't see it that way. She's constantly in their faces talking to them about something crazy, and they just ignore her. She sees herself one way and people see her totally differently. I'm sure when people meet Pauline, they'll wonder what in the world Daddy ever saw in Momma. They don't say it; it's just the way people act. It's the way they respond when they realize that Momma's my mother, and not Pauline. It's almost a shock reaction.

I know that Uncle Todd's right, but it doesn't stop me from loving my momma. I want her to stop using drugs and come home to us.

"I hear you, Uncle, but like I said, that's my momma."

"All right, all right, but I want you to think about where we're going with this."

We talk at dinner, but not about Momma. Uncle Todd doesn't mention that she showed up at school. He does everything he can not to upset Aunt Shirley.

"I think it's time we start getting rid of Jasmine's things," Aunt Shirley blurts out unexpectedly.

"Not yet," Uncle Todd responds.

"There's no need to wait, honey. It's too hard to pass that bedroom door every day, knowing that her things are in the same spot that she left them."

"No," Uncle Todd says with tears in his eyes.

Death is so strange. I thought for sure that Aunt Shirley would be the one who would never want to get rid of Jasmine's stuff.

"It's time to start thinking about what we can do with her clothes," Aunt Shirley continues. "Maybe we can give them to her sorority sisters and they can give them to needy students."

That sounds like a really good idea to me, but I don't say anything.

Uncle Todd doesn't say anything else. He just looks at his wife.

We're all silent for the rest of our dinner and during breakfast the next morning.

Silent, until Momma shows up.

I am speechless as we all watch Momma standing at the glass door in the kitchen. She looks like a homeless person.

"Please let her in," I say to Aunt Shirley and Uncle Todd as they start to look the other way.

I get up without permission and go to the door.

"Momma, come in. Are you hungry?"

"Yes, son, Momma's hungry. I haven't had food in days."

I start to ask her why she didn't buy food with the money I gave her, but I know that's a dumb question.

I get ready to pull out a chair for her to sit down, but she sits in my chair and starts eating out of my plate with her hands. She looks like a wild animal.

Uncle Todd shakes his head.

Aunt Shirley just can't stand it another minute. "Sister, what in the world is going on with you?"

Momma starts talking a mile a minute, trying to explain why she's hungry and all the details of the last few days.

"I can't find a job. Now that old crazy landlord is talking about kicking me out. I ain't got nowhere to go."

"You do have someplace to go, sister, but the drugs and Clarine have to stay out of my house."

Momma's looking at Aunt Shirley like she's crazy for real. "You saying I can come back?"

"No, you can't come back *now*. You can spend tonight, and then tomorrow you can go to rehab over in Raleigh. You can come back later when you're better."

Momma nods. "That's fair, that's fair." She says it like she's really going to do the right thing this time.

But Uncle Todd's not going along with this at all. "You can stay in the guesthouse in the back." He picks up his pilot's hat and his suitcase. He has to go to work, and he walks out the door.

"My own house? Cool."

Nothing fazes my momma. She's so busy trying to get what she can get from people that she doesn't care that she's not wanted in this house. She eats all of my food, then everything that is left on the table.

"Put my pitcher down, girl!" Aunt Shirley shouts as Momma raises a crystal water pitcher up to her mouth and drinks from it like it's a regular glass.

"You can spend the night here out in the guest-house, but I'm driving you to Raleigh tomorrow if they have a bed for you. No later than tomorrow."

"Cool," Momma says again like she's going to Disneyland.

Uncle Todd's blowing the car horn for me to come outside so that he can give me a ride to school.

I kiss Momma and Aunt Shirley before running out to the car. I can see that Uncle Todd's angry. He's trying not to let me see it, but faces do not lie.

"Do you think she'll be okay this time, Uncle Todd?" I ask him as we're driving, as if he really cares.

"I just don't know, son. I do love your momma, she's my wife's sister, but I try not to worry about her. She doesn't seem to want help. I have to be more concerned about my wife and you."

He stops talking for a moment, and I stay quiet

so that I don't say the wrong thing. "It's not that I don't care, it's just becoming too much to deal with. On top of trying to deal with losing Jasmine and the grief in your aunt's heart, it's too much."

I understand why Uncle Todd feels the way he does about Momma, but it still hurts. I often wonder how he would feel if it was his blood sister.

"I'll see you soon. I have two flights back to back. I'll be home in a few days."

"Bye, Uncle."

I can't think straight all day at school. I want to get home to see how Momma's doing. When I get home from school, I run out to the guesthouse. I open the door, but the place is empty. Where could she be? I run to the other side of the guesthouse, hoping that Momma's at the pool. Maybe she went for a walk. I go inside the main house.

I'm changing my clothes in my room when I hear a noise in the room next to me.

"Jasmine?" I run down the hall to Jasmine's room.

It's Momma. She's so busy stuffing Jasmine's jewelry in her purse that she doesn't even hear me come in.

"Momma, what are you doing? How can you steal Jasmine's things?"

"Shut up, boy. I ain't stealing. I'm just moving this stuff so that my sister won't have to do it. She's upset enough."

"*Moving* it? Why are you stuffing her jewelry in your purse? Now, put it back."

"Yes, sister, put it back." Aunt Shirley is standing at the door. "First you abandon Joseph and we take him in. Then you run in and out of my house like this is a two-dollar motel. If that's not enough, you bring that fool Bow into our lives. He kills my daughter and you helped him. Now you're stealing my baby's things!"

Aunt Shirley is trying to be angry, but her emotions take over and she falls onto her knees and sobs.

"Momma, you have to leave." I try to push her out into the hallway. I grab her purse and empty the stuff onto the floor. As if it is no big deal at all, Momma just kneels down on the floor and picks up her things, leaving Jasmine's jewelry. Then she gets up and walks out.

There's nothing I can say to Aunt Shirley. We just sit there and look at the items that Momma tried to steal. All of Jasmine's favorite things—a charm bracelet that Uncle Todd gave her, the gold necklace that I saved up money and bought her from T.J. Maxx last Christmas. Momma was even going to take the earrings that Grandma gave Jasmine when she was a little girl.

Aunt Shirley finally stops looking at the precious things. She gets up and lies across Jasmine's bed.

Without eating dinner, I fall asleep on the floor of Jasmine's room again. When I wake up, it's 6:30 in the morning. Aunt Shirley's gone. I guess she left in the middle of the night. I'm glad Uncle Todd is away on a flight. I run downstairs. Aunt Shirley is having breakfast. She's looking out the window.

"What are you looking at, Auntie?"

"Your mother."

I can't believe it. Momma had the nerve to stay in the guesthouse all night! I think the crack has really fried her brain like the commercial on television says it can. She's sitting on the front porch of the guesthouse like she's on vacation.

"What are you going to do now?" I ask my aunt as if there's really an easy answer for Momma.

"I'm having her committed today. We lost Jasmine

as a result of drugs; I'm not going to lose my sister, too. Besides, I promised Momma and Poppa that I would take care of Betty. She really is pitiful. Just look at her."

Aunt Shirley leans over in the chair in total disbelief. My aunt's heart really is made of gold. Sister or not, I'm not sure that I could forgive Momma if Jasmine was my daughter. I don't know how she can stand the sight of Momma anymore.

"Does she know she's going to rehab today?" I ask as Aunt Shirley gets up and walks to the back door.

"She'll know in a few minutes. The cops are on the way."

"The cops! You called the cops on my momma?" I stand up to go warn Momma.

"Sit down, Joseph. This is the best thing for her. I'm giving her a choice. Go to rehab or go to jail for stealing Jasmine's things."

"No, you can't do this, man!"

"*Man!* Do not refer to me as 'man,' Joseph! Sit down and do not raise your voice in this house."

I am mad at my aunt for the first time in my life. I don't want my momma to go to jail; but I also know better than to talk back to my aunt or any other adult.

Just as I'm going to start to plead with my aunt, the doorbell rings.

Aunt Shirley goes into the living room and opens the front door. I follow her and notice that she's still walking along the edge of the floor in the living room. It's been weeks since Jasmine was murdered and Aunt Shirley still refuses to step in the spot where her daughter died.

Watching her take that sad walk around the new rug is a reminder that, yes, we have to do something to help Momma. We have to do something drastic and we need to do it now.

CHAPTER SEVEN

It's hard to stand there and listen to Aunt Shirley explain to the cops what Momma did last night. They warn her that they can only help get Momma over to Raleigh, but they can't force her to go into rehab.

"What's going on in here? You called Five-O on me?" Momma shrieks as she rushes into the room like she owns the house. She has no problem at all stepping on the spot where Jasmine's lifeless body lay.

"Yes, sister, I did call the police. Not to arrest you, but to help you."

"*Help* me. How is jail going to help me?"

"You aren't going to jail. But you are going to rehab and you're going today."

"Who said that?"

"I said you're going or you're going straight to jail. Now, which will it be?"

"I did nothing wrong and you got no witness."

Momma looks at me. She thinks once again I'll lie for her. Once again she'll use me. I look at her standing there in the very spot that my poor cousin took her last breath. She's not even aware why Aunt Shirley is looking at her feet, not her face. I can't save Momma, not this time.

"I saw you, Momma. I saw you stealing Jasmine's things. You need help."

"I brought you into this world, boy, and I will take you out," Momma shouts, and she has that crazy look in her eyes again.

"Do not threaten this young man, miss," one of the police officers says.

"Threaten him? The threat is against *me*. They trying to make me go someplace I do not want to go."

The officer talks to Momma like he deals with her kind every day.

"Miss, what's it going to be? Are you going with us or are you going to the rehab center?" He takes his handcuffs out and starts walking toward Momma.

"Joseph, don't let them take me!"

There's nothing I can do as Momma starts to cry like she's going to the electric chair. Aunt Shirley's crying too, but she never takes her eyes off of Momma's feet.

"All right, all right, I will go to your damn rehab!" Momma finally yells.

Aunt Shirley and I walk behind the officers as they put Momma into the police car. I open the door to the passenger side of my aunt's car as she prepares to follow the police officers.

"You can't go, son. I want you to go to school. I'll call the principal and let him know that you're going to be late."

"No, Auntie, I have to go and make sure that Momma is all right."

"Go to school, Joseph. I mean it!"

Aunt Shirley gets in her car, and they all drive off and leave me standing there. Momma looks out the back window at me like she's a little girl. She barely raises her hand, but she manages to wave a little, and I wave back. Once again I watch Momma leaving me. My heart hurts like it did when Jasmine died.

When I get to school, I feel so alone and paranoid. I feel like the whole school knows about Momma and that everyone is laughing at me. The truth is, the people at school have no clue what's really going on. Not even Valerie, but she'll know soon enough. I hope and pray the other students have their parents at home, not in drug rehab.

"What's up, man?"

I turn around and it's Paul. I don't say anything.

"What's wrong, Joseph?" he asks with this real look of concern on his face.

"Nothing, man. I'm all right." I don't want to talk about it.

There's no way I'm going to tell him that Momma has gone to a full-time rehab center. That's what I miss about Jasmine more than anything else. I miss being able to tell her stuff about Momma. She never judged Momma.

"Never judge others," Jasmine always said. That's what she taught me.

I don't say anything to anyone all morning in my classes. It's easier to keep to myself, easier not to explain.

Unfortunately, Valerie comes over during study period, and she knows me almost as well as Jasmine did.

"What's wrong?" she asks as soon as she sits down beside me. Somehow her cute little face always makes me smile.

"Is it Miss Betty?" she asks, and waits for me to tell her the next horror story about Momma.

"Yes, it's Momma. Aunt Shirley forced her to go to rehab, and I don't know if that was the right thing to do. She has to want to go on her own."

Valerie holds my hand.

"I'm sorry that you're going through this, but I really think rehab is what Miss Betty needs now more than anything."

Changing the subject, she smiles at me again. "Come on, don't be sad. Let's go to the movies Friday night. You need to hang out more!"

"Sounds good." We open our books to study.

I spend the next two days worrying about Momma, but I'm also getting ready for my date with Valerie and working on my tennis game.

Aunt Shirley tells me that the doctors at the facility say it will be a little while before Momma can have visitors, so there's not much I can do. Maybe I can visit her next week if Aunt Shirley will drive me to Raleigh.

Friday night can't come fast enough for me. I want to spend some fun time with Valerie away from Target and school.

Trying to be Mr. Independent, I catch the bus to the movie theater. I don't want my girl to see me catching a ride for our date. Of course Aunt Shirley gave me a long lecture this morning when I told her I was going to the movies after tennis practice. She told me the same stuff Daddy and Uncle Todd have said a thousand times. "Be respectful. Save sex for marriage."

Valerie is standing at her mother's car door, and it looks like Ms. Monet is giving her a lecture too.

"Hi, Ms. Monet. Hi, Valerie."

Ms. Monet gives me the look that only a mother can give her daughter's boyfriend.

"Hello, Joseph." She gives me a half smile and a handshake. "How are your folks doing?"

"They are doing a little better. Thanks for asking."

She looks at us both again, tells us to have a good time, and drives off.

We rush inside to get tickets for the movie, but to our surprise, it's sold out.

"What now?" Valerie asks.

"Let's walk to Aunt Shirley's and watch a movie there. She's gotta be home by now. I'm sure she won't mind us hanging out with her."

Hand in hand I walk with Valerie all the way back to my folks' house. But when we get there, my aunt's car isn't in the driveway. Uncle Todd and Aunt Shirley stopped parking in the three-car garage after Jasmine died so that they wouldn't have to look at her car every day.

"Maybe we shouldn't go in," Valerie says as I unlock the door.

"It's all right. I'll just tell them the truth, that the movie was sold out."

"Look, here's a note." Valerie picks it up and reads aloud. "'I left you several voice mails while you were in practice. Gone to Raleigh to see your mother. I am spending the night because Todd has a layover. I thought we would have a late dinner. He's flying out again tomorrow. I'll be back around ten o'clock in the morning.'"

"I thought your momma couldn't have visitors," Valerie wonders aloud.

"That's what all the grown-ups said. I guess

they're just trying to get me focused on school and off Momma." I pause. "Looks like we got the house to ourselves."

"I don't know about this, Joseph. I really think I should go."

"Nope, come on, let's watch a movie."

We sit down in the den and watch a movie and laugh. It feels good to laugh again, especially with Valerie.

When the movie's over, Valerie gets up to leave. "It's getting late," she says.

I don't know what comes over me, but I can't help myself as I stand up and kiss her on the mouth. I have kissed girls before, but kissing Valerie is different. Our kiss turns into more kissing, and we lie down on the couch together.

"Are you a virgin?" she asks like she is expecting me to say yes.

I lie.

"Of course not." That's what guys are supposed to say. At least, that's what I think I'm supposed to say.

"Are *you* a virgin?" I ask.

"Yes, and I'm going to stay one until I'm ready, so let's just watch television, okay?"

I'm kind of glad that she's turned me down. My daddy would be proud of me. He's made me promise him a thousand times that I won't have sex until I'm older and have discussed it with him.

After all of that drama we make the mistake of falling asleep while waiting for the next HBO movie to come on.

"Oh my God, my mother is going to kill me!" Valerie jumps up and straightens out her clothes in a total panic. We run to her folks' house as fast as we can.

Thank God they're not home yet.

I run back home and jump into bed, praying that my aunt hasn't called. I think about Valerie for the rest of the night. I have no way of knowing how I'm supposed to feel now. Our kisses seemed so serious. But what now? I just know she's pretty and smart and I like her. And I think she likes me.

I feel strange the next morning, as if I've done something really bad like Momma. I think I might've been too aggressive with Valerie. I hope not. I hope Valerie knows I'll always respect her and her wishes.

I don't know what to say or do when Aunt Shirley walks in the door.

"Did you two have a good time at the movies?" she asks before she even mentions Momma.

"Yes," I lie. "How's Momma?"

"She's very sick, Joseph. But she will be fine if she completes the program. They're going to help her."

Aunt Shirley gives me a hug and goes to her room.

I do my Saturday chores and I think about Momma and Valerie.

I'm so glad that I didn't cross the line with Valerie. I don't want to lie and deceive people like Momma is always doing. I don't want to be that kind of person. I have to at least tell Daddy what happened with Valerie. He'll be glad to know that I didn't cross the line with her and respected her feelings.

I wonder if I'm supposed to call Valerie. I just hope she's not too upset with me for being a little pushy.

Before I can call her, my cell phone rings. It's Valerie!

"Hi, Joseph."

"Hi, Valerie. Look, I'm sorry about last night. I hope you're not upset with me."

"I love you, Joseph. You're my friend and we both

know we are too young for sex." She says it like she really means it.

"I love you, too." I say it like I understand what's going on between us. The thing I know for sure is that my father's right. I am too young for sex. One long kiss and we are talking about love.

All weekend I think about what a nice girlfriend I have. I think about how Aunt Shirley is always saying that Momma wasn't always the way she is now. I'm sure Momma used to be a nice girl just like Valerie is. Just like Jasmine was. I don't know what happened to Momma.

Uncle Todd gets in from his flight early Sunday morning, and Aunt Shirley announces that we are going over to Raleigh to see Momma after church. I think Auntie feels bad about telling me that Momma couldn't have visitors. She's not a liar like Momma. Uncle Todd declares himself too tired to go to church or to Raleigh. Aunt Shirley and I are on our own for this one.

I don't much like coming to this church anymore because I keep seeing Jasmine's body lying in her casket at the altar. I wouldn't dare mention that to Aunt Shirley.

After church I find myself feeling excited. I don't know if it's because Valerie came to church too or because I'm on my way to see Momma, or maybe a little of both.

"This place looks like a prison camp," I say to Aunt Shirley as we drive up to the rehab center. It's one big, flat building. It doesn't have bars anywhere, but the fence is really high and security is everywhere.

"I'm sure it feels like a prison to the people who are inside," Aunt Shirley replies as she reaches over and rubs my hand. "It's going to be all right, son. I promise."

We get out of the car and walk slowly to the front door arm in arm. I think we're holding each other up.

A female security guard checks Aunt Shirley's bag and directs us to the waiting area. All the patients have the same look on their faces that Momma has when she's getting treatment. They all look like this is their last time doing drugs, but that has never been true for Momma.

I look around at all the mothers, fathers, and children trying to get help for their loved ones. It doesn't take long for Momma to come out of her room. I'm shocked to see how much smaller she is. She has that look of desperation on her face again. The look that she wants someone to help her, to save her. Almost like a child in trouble.

"I hate the food here!" Momma cries as she walks toward me. "Joseph, I hate the food!"

I hug her and rub her hair. She looks a little better, just thin.

"It's going to be all right, Momma," I say, like I am really sure this time she'll recover and come home to us. That's all I can say. I'm just tired of being her father. I don't know what else to do. We all sit down. My mind wanders in and out as Momma and Aunt Shirley talk about the program at the facility.

I think about Valerie and what happened on Friday night. I think about how happy Jasmine would be to know that Momma is getting help.

When it's time to say good-bye to Momma, she's very upset with us.

"Don't leave me, Joseph," she sobs.

"We're coming back soon, Momma. Please don't cry."

Momma is getting so upset that Aunt Shirley has to ask security to take her back to her room. One thing's for sure, Aunt Shirley has had enough of Momma's mess. She's very serious about her changing her life, even if Momma isn't.

I wish Momma loved herself as much as Aunt Shirley loves her. As much as I love her!

Momma kicks and screams as the aides guide her very carefully back to her room.

"Don't turn around," Aunt Shirley says as she holds my arm tight. "Keep walking."

As we travel home, Aunt Shirley just sings along with her Shirley Caesar CD and I join in. When we turn the car onto Highway 40, Aunt Shirley finally reaches over and turns the volume down.

"Son, you don't have to go back to the rehab center if you don't want to. That's no place for a child."

"No, it's okay. I want to see my momma. I want to know how she's doing and I want her to know that I love her. I just don't understand why she's so angry at me all the time."

"She's not mad at you, Joseph. She's mad at the world. And she's mad at herself. Like all of us, she has some guilt about what happened to Jasmine."

"Why do you feel guilty, Aunt Shirley? You didn't do anything wrong."

I look down at my cell phone. It's vibrating and I see it's Valerie for the third time in the past hour. I know better than to answer around Aunt Shirley. She pays everything I do a little too much attention. She'll pick up right away on what happened between me and Valerie.

My mind has kind of drifted away from what Aunt Shirley is saying.

"Joseph, are you listening to me?"

"Yes, ma'am. I'm listening."

"Well, a mother is supposed to always protect her child, Joseph. I don't feel I did that. I always wonder if things would've been different if we had arrived five minutes earlier. I would have taken that bullet for my baby, you know."

I don't say anything after she says that. Because I think like that all the time. That crazy Bow would have killed us all if he'd had the opportunity. I just know that there's nothing I can do to bring my cousin back. Nothing!

As soon as we get in the house, I call Valerie.

"Where have you been?"

"I went to see Momma."

I'm glad I said that, because Valerie stops sounding mad when I tell her that we went to Raleigh. I have to admit, I'm not sure what to say or do now that we've become a real couple. Is this what heavy kissing does to a relationship? If so, I better stop now, because we don't really know what we're doing.

"Are you coming over here?"

"I have to ask my aunt."

"Ask me what?" Aunt Shirley asks as she walks past my door.

"It's Valerie. She'd like for me to come over to her house for a little while."

"You guys were hanging out Friday night and at school all week. How about spending this afternoon on your homework for tomorrow?"

No need to argue with Aunt Shirley. I say good-bye to Valerie and get on the computer to finish a science project.

The next day at school Valerie seems a little mad again.

I guess this is what my daddy means about getting too serious too young. I don't know how I'm supposed to treat her, but I know she's looking for something totally different than what we had last week.

What am I going to do? I think as I sit beside her in study hall.

"Are you all right today?" I ask as she pulls her desk closer to my desk so that we can study together.

"I'm fine, but I'm a little upset that we couldn't hang out yesterday. I wanted to see you."

Valerie is not a clingy person, so I think she's as confused as I am about us and this new girlfriend/ boyfriend thing.

"I'm sorry too, but you know how Aunt Shirley is when it comes to homework."

Nothing seems to ease her mind.

That's the way Valerie is for a few days. She's just tripping.

"What's really wrong?" I finally ask her.

"Nothing's wrong. It just seems like you spend all your time with your aunt and at the rehab center. I don't think you have time for a girlfriend."

She looks really sad when she says that.

And I realize that maybe I need to try to get back to being Valerie's good friend without too much romantic involvement.

"I'm sorry, Val. I'm just really worried about my momma."

"I understand, Joseph. I can't imagine my momma taking drugs and us not having a place to live." Valerie is so much like Jasmine. She is so mature. Much more than I am. "Let's just be friends for now," she adds with a smile.

"Yeah, I think that's best," I say. "But no dating other dudes," I add.

We both laugh.

CHAPTER EIGHT

After three weeks of school and practice every day, it's time for my first tennis match. It's somewhat of a sad day because I still can't erase Jasmine's death from my mind. I can't stop thinking about my cousin and the fact that she won't be in the stands today to cheer me on. Daddy is still serving in Iraq, and Momma is still in rehab, where she should be.

Uncle Todd canceled his flight today so that he could be here for my first tennis match, and Aunt Shirley is planning to leave her office early. I'm surprised to see them at warm-up practice, though.

"What are you guys doing here so early?"

"This may not be the best time to tell you this, Joseph, but we don't want someone else to tell you first." My aunt speaks with a serious look on her face.

"Did something happen to Momma?"

"No, but Bow was finally caught by the police today. Over by Henry Homes, and that means there'll be a trial. A trial that you will have to testify at as the star witness."

Aunt Shirley and Uncle Todd assure me that everything's going to be all right, and I believe them. I'm not going to let Bow scare me like he used to scare Jasmine.

"You all right?" Uncle Todd asks.

"Yes, and thanks for telling me. Oh, look, Valerie got here. Can I be excused to say hello?"

"Go ahead, son. Good luck in your match. We

will talk more tonight," Aunt Shirley says as she gives me a big hug.

I stop to talk to Valerie for a few minutes before going into the tennis match. She seems happier today because we have been hanging out a little more—but no serious stuff, just hanging out. Valerie and I just want to enjoy school and being teenagers. She wants to help me get through this difficult time. I decide not to tell her about Bow until later. She's just as afraid of him as Jasmine used to be. I don't want to upset her.

We lose the tennis match, but I'm so happy to see my family in the stands cheering for me. Coach says I did a good job today.

All the way home Aunt Shirley looks at me in the rearview mirror as Uncle Todd drives.

"What's wrong, Joseph?"

"Nothing, Auntie. I just know I had a bad game today."

"You did fine, son, considering all that's happened," Uncle Todd says with a smile.

Saturday morning Aunt Shirley is up early and ready to go to see Momma. When we drive up to the hospital, I have that same sick feeling inside that I always get when I come here. I'm anxious to see Momma and pray that she's better, but I hate coming here.

"Hey, Momma." I hug her tight. She wraps one arm around Aunt Shirley and the other one around me. She appears to be very calm this week and she looks so much better, but she's far from recovered.

The conversation between her and Aunt Shirley soon turns to Bow. Momma doesn't look at all surprised that Bow's been caught. I can tell she already knows exactly what's been going on.

"How do you know Bow's been arrested?" Aunt Shirley asks.

"Oh, Clarine came to visit yesterday and she told me."

Of course Aunt Clarine would rush up to the rehab center with her pimp boyfriend to give Momma the news first. Aunt Clarine can carry bad news better than a supermodel can carry a purse.

"Oh, Momma, I wish you'd stop seeing her while you're here. She's not good for you at all. She's just not going to help you or herself."

Aunt Shirley doesn't say anything. She just shakes her head as she walks over to the front desk. This gives me a chance to talk to Momma alone.

I don't get into any deep conversation with her; I just want to enjoy my short visit with her. She seems happy that we came today.

"Momma, seriously. I want you to stop spending time with Aunt Clarine. She's not related to us and she's not your friend."

Momma doesn't say anything. She just looks at me like it might be starting to sink in about Aunt Clarine.

When it's time for us to leave, she's not as upset as usual. Each visit gets a little better, but I don't think I'll ever get used to this place.

I promise Momma that we'll be back next weekend.

"Do you think she's better?" I ask Aunt Shirley when we get into the car.

"Yes, much better. This hospital's the best place for her. Maybe she can come home in a month or two."

I'm glad to hear Aunt Shirley talk about Momma coming home. After all that Momma has done to everyone, it's a miracle that she has a family left to come home to at all.

"I really don't think Aunt Clarine should be coming to see Momma. She's just bad news."

"Not to worry, son. I told the nurses that Clarine's name should be taken off of the visitation list immediately."

"Oh, that's good. That's real good," I say as I think about Aunt Clarine filling Momma's head with foolishness.

Aunt Shirley seems unfazed by Aunt Clarine and Bow at this point. Her goal is to keep them both away from Momma. She works for the top law firm in Durham, and it's safe to say she knows what the system here has in store for crazy Bow. Every judge in this area was at the funeral, and I'm sure they're waiting for Bow to come into their courtroom. Not just for murdering my cousin, but for all the other bad things he's done over the years. We're just learning that he has a rap sheet from Durham to New York. Maybe this is what Grandma was referring to whenever she said, just before punishing me, "Boy, I am going to get you for old and new."

I think the judge'll get Bow for all of his old and new bad deeds. At least, I hope so.

I'm glad that I did not tell Momma that I have to testify against Bow soon. I just don't want Momma thinking and worrying about that man and what he did. She needs to focus on herself and her family. We're all she has in the world.

CHAPTER NINE

"It's been eight weeks, Joseph," Aunt Shirley says as she drives me home from school. "I really think Betty is doing better. Much better."

"Does that mean it's time for Momma to come home?" I ask with excitement.

"Yes, it's time for her to come home. I'm not sure where home is to her, but she's welcome to stay in the guesthouse for a while. It's too much for your momma to stay in the house with Todd. He's still upset with her."

"Why aren't you upset, Aunt Shirley? She is partly responsible for Jasmine's death."

"I just can't carry that burden with me, son. It's too much. It's easier to focus on the good times I had with my daughter. If I think about how she died and all the reasons, I could just go crazy."

As we pull into the driveway, I look at her gentle face and think how lucky I am that she's my aunt.

"You know that your momma still has a long way to go." Aunt Shirley turns to face me. "I don't want you to think that she's fully recovered. Her coming home only means she won't be in a full-time live-in facility anymore. She still has to go to her meetings and take drug tests every week."

"I understand."

"No, Joseph. I don't think you do understand. More important than anything, you cannot live with her. You have to stay with us no matter what."

"Okay. I understand that, too. I really do." I kiss her and I rush into the house to sit by the telephone. Daddy is supposed to call today. I think about what Aunt Shirley said as I wait for him to call. I seriously do understand. I don't want to live with Momma anymore. I don't want to start over again. I want to have a normal home like other kids.

Daddy promised he was going to call at 5:00 p.m. and he does. We talk for a few minutes and he promises to call again soon. Never one to talk too bad about Momma, he asks me to be careful and not to expect her to recover overnight. I know that he's right, because she has disappointed me so many times.

The adults do not get it! I love my momma, but I'm seeing how bad my life is going to be if I try to be her father when she comes home.

Daddy is really concerned about the upcoming trial for crazy Bow and the fact that I have to testify. The adults are still a lot more concerned about Bow than I am. I plan to just tell the truth. The truth will put Bow away for a long time. I just know that it will.

Uncle Todd and Aunt Shirley are up early this Monday morning, and I hear them in the kitchen discussing the arraignment for Bow. They both seem a lot more upset than I am. Maybe that's because they have to give statements too. They both saw Bow running down the street away from their house minutes after Jasmine was shot.

"Good morning, son," Aunt Shirley says when I sit down for breakfast.

"Good morning." I look into her eyes to see how she's really doing.

"Are you nervous about testifying today, Joseph?" my uncle asks, as we begin to rush through breakfast so that we won't be late for court.

"No, sir, I'm not nervous. I just want to get this over with."

"Do you understand that this is an arraignment, not an actual trial?" my aunt asks.

I nod. She's explained to me about fifty times that there's a hearing to confirm that the judge has enough evidence on Bow to formally charge him and move forward with a trial.

"Yes, I understand everything and I'm ready."

There's no way I am going to tell them that I'm nervous. I want my aunt to know that I'm going to do what I need to do to make sure that Bow never hurts anyone again.

Never!

• • •

When we get to the courthouse, I'm surprised to see reporters everywhere. The *Raleigh News and Observer* has run a story about my cousin almost every week since she was killed, but today I see lots of reporters and television crews from other nearby cities.

"Keep walking and don't talk to any reporters," Uncle Todd says. He grasps my hand and holds Aunt Shirley around the waist as we walk into the courthouse and make our way to courtroom B.

The courtroom is filled with people, including Valerie and Ms. Monet. Wow, Ms. Monet's *never* let Valerie miss school before. Maybe she likes me after all. More important than liking me, I know that Ms. Monet wants to be there for my entire family. We all exchange quiet hellos as my family and I sit down in front of Valerie and Ms. Monet.

"All rise," a sheriff says as the judge enters the courtroom.

The judge is not one of the judges that I remember from the funeral or the repast. I recall that my aunt said they were bringing in a judge from another county because all of the judges in the Raleigh/Durham area know her too well and would be biased.

After the sheriff gives us instructions, we all sit down and wait. A few minutes after we take our seats, two officers bring in Bow, shackled like a dog. He killed my cousin, but it's pretty awful to see him with chains on. Horrible to see any man like that.

Aunt Shirley tenses up and cries out loud when she sees him. "You killed my baby!" she yells as Uncle Todd tries to quiet her down.

Just seeing Bow again brings back so many bad memories for me. I can't imagine how Uncle Todd and Aunt Shirley feel right now. I feel sick to my stomach.

One by one we are called to the witness stand.

The district attorney is trying to be gentle, but everything he asks makes me think of that horrible day.

"Joseph, is the man who shot your cousin Jasmine sitting in this courtroom today?"

"Yes, sir," I answer.

"Please point him out."

I point at Bow.

"No further questions." The district attorney sits down.

The judge asks the public defender if he has any questions for me. He says no just like Aunt Shirley said he would.

I'm about to get up, but I feel I have more to say.

"Your Honor, may I say something?" I ask.

"Yes, young man. Say whatever you want to say."

I take a deep breath and look at Bow sitting in front of me with this smile on his face, like he doesn't have a care in the world. I can see all the evil in his eyes that Jasmine used to talk about. He could care less that she's dead. The only emotion he has shown today was when he turned around to wave at his family.

I guess Bow got his craziness from them, because they are sitting back there laughing and carrying on like they're at a picnic.

I can't let him get away with killing our Jasmine.

I'm scared, but I can do this. I clear my throat and say, "I just want to say that I loved my cousin. Aunt Shirley and Uncle Todd loved her. My daddy loved her. And even with all of her problems, my momma loved Jasmine too. I don't understand trials and all, but I know right from wrong. I know when somebody has committed a crime. Bow did not just commit a crime, he killed someone special, sir. He killed our Jasmine. Please do not let him go free. He was my momma's boyfriend. I don't need to ever see him again to tell you that he's the man that shot my cousin in the head. He's the man that tried to destroy our family, sir."

I look over at Aunt Shirley and she smiles at me like she's very proud. Uncle Todd smiles too and nods at me.

Ms. Monet is hugging Valerie and they're both crying.

The judge looks at my aunt and then he looks at me. "Thank you. Is there anything you would like to add, young man?"

"No, sir. That's all I have to say."

The judge excuses me from the bench, and I go back to sit with my family.

When I walk by Bow, he isn't smiling anymore. For the first time all morning he looks afraid. He has every right to be afraid.

The judge looks at Bow's family, still smiling and chatting like they could care less. He looks at Bow.

"Please stand, Mr. Tann," the judge says, and gestures to the sheriff. With a sheriff on each side of him, Bow stands up, and I can see him shaking from behind.

"Mr. Frank Tann, with the evidence before me, I find that we have more than enough evidence to charge you with second degree murder and no bond will be set. Sheriff, please remove this man from the courtroom."

"Oh hell na'll," one of Bow's family members shouts.

No one in my family says a word.

Bow is led away without being allowed to say anything to his family. Not even good-bye. He doesn't deserve to talk to them. He sure didn't give my folks a chance to say good-bye to Jasmine.

"You did a good job, son," Uncle Todd says as we all walk back to the car.

On the drive home we talk about Jasmine. We talk about Grandma and Granddaddy. We talk about family. No matter what Bow tried to do to us, we are still a family.

Aunt Shirley lets me take the afternoon off from school, and Valerie stays home too. We all have lunch together at Aunt Shirley's. After lunch Ms. Monet lets Valerie stay at our house because she has to get to work. Uncle Todd leaves for a short flight, but he seems so relieved.

We have a nice time together. Having Valerie in the house reminds me of old times with Jasmine.

Happy times.

CHAPTER TEN

I've been sleeping good knowing that Bow will be going to jail, but I didn't sleep a wink last night. I was too excited to sleep. It's Saturday morning, and we're going to Raleigh to get Momma from the rehab center and bring her home.

Maybe she'll finally learn how to deal with her problems and we can be a family like we used to be. There's nothing I would like more than to see her happy again.

"Come and get your breakfast, Joseph," Aunt

Shirley calls from the kitchen. "It's almost time to leave."

Uncle Todd must have come home early from his trip, because I think I hear another voice coming from downstairs. I smile as I think about how long it's been since I've heard Aunt Shirley sound so happy about anything. She hasn't smiled much since the summer, and it was as if she would never smile again.

I run down the stairs.

"Daddy!"

I fall into my father's arms. It was not Uncle Todd's voice that I heard. It's Daddy. My daddy is back home.

"Son, it is so good to see you."

"What are you doing here? You told me you weren't sure when your assignment would end."

"I know, but my tour of duty is over. I wanted to surprise you."

"I'm so happy, Daddy!"

"I think they just got tired of your old man and sent me home for good. I'm sorry I didn't get home in time for the arraignment. I heard you did great."

Of course, Aunt Shirley knew for days that Daddy was coming and she never said a word. She comes in from the kitchen and stands right in the spot where Jasmine died and holds on to Daddy like he's her own blood brother.

We all hug. I'm so glad to see my daddy. He kept his promise. He came home to me.

We all go into the kitchen to have breakfast together. The laughter at the table is as sweet as seeing Daddy again.

Daddy decides he'll ride with us to Raleigh to get Momma.

Just as we're getting into the car, the telephone rings. "Oh, I wonder what D.A. Rollin wants on a

Saturday morning," Aunt Shirley says as she looks at the caller ID.

She answers the telephone and begins to laugh and cry at the same time. Then she hangs up.

"Bow is pleading guilty to second-degree murder. He's agreeing to life in prison without a trial."

As horrible as a life sentence sounds, we're all glad. I really don't want my aunt to have to sit through a trial and look at that man again. None of us should ever have to look at his sorry behind again in life.

Everything is going to be all right, I think as we pull up to the gate of the rehab center for what I really hope is the last time.

But then I see Aunt Clarine's Toyota in the parking lot with the big dice hanging from the rearview mirror. Somehow she has found out that Momma's being released and she's here too. Why is that not a surprise? It's just too good to be true that we can have a family gathering without Aunt Clarine interfering. Leave it to Aunt Clarine to get into the center, even after Aunt Shirley told the nurses to take her name off the list. She's in the waiting room with Momma when we walk in.

"Child, I came to pick you up," Aunt Clarine says to Momma as she pops her gum and rolls her eyes at Daddy.

Aunt Shirley and Daddy just totally ignore Aunt Clarine.

"Looks like you lost a pound or two," Aunt Clarine says to Aunt Shirley, hoping to start an argument.

"Clarine, girl, thanks for coming," Momma says quickly, "but I think I'll go with my sister today."

"Sister, *I'm* your sister," Aunt Clarine says as she rolls her eyes at Aunt Shirley and starts to walk away, with Ellsworth following her. "I'll be in the car waiting for you, girl," she adds, as if she thinks Momma is joking about riding home with us.

Daddy doesn't say anything. He keeps his arm around my shoulder. I think his joy is just in knowing that his brother is no longer married to that horrible woman and that Momma may finally be getting clean.

All I can think about is Valerie and how fortunate we are that we know better than to get too serious too soon. She's a beautiful girl, and when I become a man, I would want her in my life, not a nutcase like Aunt Clarine. Right now I just want to enjoy school, my friends, and Valerie. I want to enjoy my parents sitting in this car together, riding home without having a fight. Of course, Momma's rolling her eyes like Aunt Clarine when Daddy starts talking to Pauline on his cell phone. She may as well stop that mess, because she knows Daddy isn't thinking about her other than as my mother. When we have a chance alone, I'll have to put Momma in check about that baby mama drama stuff.

I wake up bright and early the next morning. I am too excited to sleep. Uncle Todd came home last night. He and Daddy played chess most of the night while I watched them. I'm trying to learn the game too. Momma and Aunt Shirley were in Jasmine's room packing her things until about 2 a.m. Daddy slept in the room with me when we finally went to bed. He says he's going to buy us a condo so that I won't have to change schools again. That's my pops. Always thinking about me first.

Everyone seems so happy this morning. Uncle Todd even goes out of his way to be nice to Momma when she walks up from the guesthouse for breakfast.

I see her walking across the grass and I run over to meet her.

"Good morning, Momma."

"Good morning. It's a nice day."

"It's nice because you're home. Are you staying this time, Momma? Are you really going to be all right?"

Momma looks at me and gives me a big hug like she used to years ago. "Momma's going to work on staying clean. I pray to God that we're never apart again."

"You mean until I get married."

Momma stops hugging me and lets out a big laugh. A laugh I had almost forgotten.

We walk hand in hand to Aunt Shirley's kitchen, where everybody is waiting for us. We usually leave Jasmine's chair empty, but today Daddy sits in her seat and it's all right. It's really all right.

After eating a good breakfast, we all pile into Daddy's rental van and go to church together as a family.

As soon as Momma realizes that Miss Pauline's at church waiting for Daddy, she frowns a little, but that's okay too. That's just one more thing for her to get over. Momma's rehab is helping all of us. She is going to be all right. She really is.

And if things are not all right, Miss Novella Edmonds makes it all right when she stands up and starts singing.

"Amazing grace! How sweet the sound
That saved a wretch like me!
I once was lost, but now am found . . ."

Then Reverend Davis stands up. "The doors of the church are open. If anybody would like to join as a candidate for baptism or by Christian experience, come. Come now. Jesus is waiting for you."

Miss Novella just keeps on singing.

I feel the body next to me moving. I have to open my eyes so that I can see for myself. It's Momma. My momma is rejoining church after all of these years. Aunt Shirley stands up and shouts like Grandma used to before she died. Uncle Todd claps his hands.

"Thank you, Lord, thank you," Aunt Shirley shouts.

Daddy says, "Amen."

Miss Pauline cries.

Aunt Clarine is in the back of the church screaming like she's lost her mind. Again!

Momma doesn't stop walking, and when she finally reaches the altar, it's like she's come home again. She falls down at the feet of the preacher like she's just met Jesus. Then I realize that maybe she has.

I don't see Jasmine's body lying across the front of the church in her casket anymore. I see Daddy safe at home with us. I see my momma changing her life to be drug-free. I see a normal life for me.

Momma is praying and shouting along with half the women in the church.

"Momma," I say aloud. She's come back to me. She has come back to us all.

Miss Novella just keeps on singing. I join in with her.

"'Amazing grace! How sweet the sound . . .'"

ACKNOWLEDGMENTS

The longer I write, the less I take my life for granted. Each book has its challenges and I learn a new song with every paragraph. What I never forget are the people who are with me on the journey. Thank you, Emma Dryden, my editor and friend. This is our sixth book together, and it seems like just yesterday that we worked on *The Legend of Buddy Bush*. Edward Necarsulmer, you are young, with the wisdom of an eighty-year-old man. I appreciate you as my agent and friend. I appreciate all the people at McIntosh & Otis and Simon & Schuster for their support over the years.

What is life without family and friends? You know who you are and you know that I love you all. Most of all, I am so grateful to God for his love and forgiveness. And to my mother, Maless Moses. I can hear her prayers eight hundred miles away.